Mark Allen

The Mystery of Ardennes, Le mystère d'Ardennes

A drama in five acts

Mark Allen

The Mystery of Ardennes, Le mystère d'Ardennes
A drama in five acts

ISBN/EAN: 9783337343798

Printed in Europe, USA, Canada, Australia, Japan

Cover: Foto ©Andreas Hilbeck / pixelio.de

More available books at **www.hansebooks.com**

THE

MYSTERY OF ARDENNES,

Le Mystere d'Ardennes.

A DRAMA

IN FIVE ACTS,

BY MARK ALLEN;

Author of "Ranting Moll," "Wayaniko,"
"Tory Renegade," "Courier of the Czar,"
"A Crucial Trial," etc. etc.

WOBURN, MASS.
PRINTED AT THE ADVERTISER OFFICE,
1888.

DRAMATIS PERSONÆ.

— ·:⊙(⊙:·· —

Characters represented in First, Second, and Third Acts.

M. DUBOIS, a wealthy Contractor, Maire of Solenthel.
M. JARVAIS, his Secretary aged 75 years.
M. MESNARD, Collector of Taxes, adjoint to the Maire.
DENNIS O'GRADY, in the Service of Dubois.
M. HENRI DE PIERREPONT, Successor to Mesnard.
M. DUMONT, Landlord of the Soliel d'Or.
M. LAROQUE, Agent of Police.
PRESIDENT OF THE COURT.
MARIE DE PIERREPONT, wife of Henri.
MADELEINE DE PIERREPONT, age 7 years.
Associate Judges, Jurors, Counsellors, Officers of the Court, Gen d'Armes, Waiters, Servants, Villagers.

Characters represented in Fourth and Fifth Acts.

M. GAILLARD, a wealthy Merchant of Lima, Peru.
ARTHUR DE VERSAN, a young Lawyer.
M LAROSE, } Merchants, friends of DeVersan.
M CLEVEL, }
DENNIS O'GRADY, the same unfortunate, some fourteen years older.
M. DUMONT, Landlord of the Soldiel d'Or.
M JARVAIS, aged 90 years.
FRANCOIS, valet to M. Gaillard.
PHYSICIAN.
HENRI dePEIRREPONT, a pardoned Convict.
MARIE dePEIRREPONT, an outcast, Wife of Henri.
MADELEINE dePEIRREPONT, their daughter, aged 22 yrs.

THE MYSTERY OF ARDENNES.

ACT FIRST.

SCENE. I.—*Bureau of M. Dubois.* (THE MOTIVE.)
An old-fashioned room with C. *door opening into room
beyond. Writing tables* R. H. & L. H. *Old-fashioned
chairs; easy-chair* R. C.

Discovered—M. DUBOIS *seated in easy-chair* R. C.
JARVAIS *seated, writing,* R. H. DENNIS O'GRADY, R.
of C. D. *with feather duster in hand.*

Dubois Well Dennis, have you finished?

Dennis. Yes your honor; I've dusted all the books
and the furnitoor.

Dub. You may retire.

Den. You mane I may lave?

Dub. Yes leave us now.

Den. That's aisy done your honor. But when will
I come back?

Dub. When I ring for you.

Den. You'll ring the little bell there when you
want me will you?

Dub. Yes, yes, begone. [*Exit* DENNIS, C. D. R.
That Irishman has an honest heart but an excessive
command of language; his ready wit and good hu-
mor amuses me, yet he carries it to such extremes
at times that I become vexed and sometimes, almost
lose my temper.

Jarvais. In taking him in and giving him a home
and an opportunity to earn a livelihood, you have
done a good act and given another evidence of your
generous heart, M. Dubois.

Dub. That will do Jarvais; to business. So M.
Mesnard continues his dissolute course of life?

Jarvais. Yes, M. Dubois he does; such a person
is entirely unfitted for, and unworthy the important
trusts you have committed to him; his nights are

spent in dissipation and at the gaming table and he squanders large sums in a manner unbecoming your collector.

Dub. It grieves me good Jarvais to hear such reports. I have had my suspicions aroused before this. Mesnard's fortune is ample — still such a course as he is pursuing must eventually lead to ruin and disgrace.

Jar. You say truly. Monsieur, you who have always been a strict economist, and, though by some called close and penurious, honest and upright in all your dealings, have sufficient knowledge of human nature as well as the proprieties of public life to realize the fact that with the heavy responsibilities resting upon you, you must have those about you whose habits are above suspicion.

Dub. Jarvais, you are an old and faithful secretary and a true friend. I like your frankess ; you speak your honest thoughts and I like you for it. It is true that those who know me not, regard me as close and miserly ; perhaps I give them occasion. Although possessed of wealth I have lived a frugal life ; I have despised extravagance and foolish display, and have not squandered my income in folly and vice. I have been saving, very saving, and have not been the votary of folly and fashion. I have saved that I might do good. I say this to you, Jarvais, because you are my confidante, I say it not to every one. I have helped those that have needed help ; yet, I have not allowed a trumpet to be sounded before me but in giving alms have endeavored to carry out the precept, "Let not thy left hand know what thy right hand doeth."

Jar. Good, M. Dubois, I know you to be generous and kind, and there are many that would have suffered had it not been for your kind offices dispensed with secrecy.

Dub. Say no more Jarvais ; I seek no praise of men. Let my inward consciousness of having done my duty by my fellow men be my reward here and in the future may I have the satisfaction of learning

that I have something credited to my account in the
great treasury above. But of Mesnard—

Jar. True, your affairs, the rents, the taxes are
not safe in his hands; he lacks principle; and in
lacking that he lacks everything. It is time there
was a change.

Dub. Yes, 'tis time there was a change, summon
him here at once. I will dismiss him. I will no
longer assume such a risk. [*Jarvais has risen and
about to retire.*] But stay; who can fill his place?

Jar. Does no one suggest himself? Think!

Dub. I can think of no one, Jarvais.

Jar. Then allow me to suggest the name of M.
Henri de Pierrepont. He is poor, though descended
from a noble family; but above all he is honest and
trustworthy. With such a man you could feel secure;
believe me you can trust him.

Dub. My faithful Jarvais; why did I not think of
him before? His father was my friend and this
Henri I have known from a child. His father was
a man after my own heart, Jarvais. He was scrupu-
lously honest; he was a man of temperate and frugal
habits; not given to extravagance and show. Such
men are rare, and I like them. I have observed this
Henri; and he seems so like his father that I shall
not hesitate to offer him the position. He has a
wife and one child, I understand; he has also some
employment as a collector of rents for a rich relative
which, I suspect gives him but slight support. I
warrant he does not indulge in many luxuries. What
he will receive, added to his present income, will ena-
ble him and his family to live comfortably. See M.
de Pierrepont good Jarvais and inform him of my
wishes.

Jar. Depend upon me M. Dubois.

[*Exit* JARVAIS, C. D. L.

Dub. [*Solus.*] I will no longer give countenance
to such dissipation and extravagance; Mesnard needs
not the position. He has ample means of his own.
I will give it to one who will appreciate it, and whom
it will benefit. Jarvais is everything to me; eyes,
ears, perception too. He relieves me of half my

burdens: he has grown gray in my service, and his fidelity shall not be forgotten. I hate extravagance; dissolute habits I despise. The gamester and the libertine are my great abhorence. This Mesnard, in whom I have trusted and confided has become a source of great anxiety to me. Twice I have given him to understand that his course of life is known to me, and have warned him of the result, yet he received it coldly and shows no signs of mending. Here our relations must end. I will have done with him forever.

[*Enter* MESNARD, C. D. L.

Dub. Good day M. Mesnard.

Mesnard. Your servant, M. Dubois. You have sent for me; how can I serve you?

Dub. You look somewhat pale and haggard, M. Mesnard.

Mes. I suppose it is the effect of too much mental labor; too many business cares M. Dubois.

Dub. M. Mesnard, I am a plain, blunt man; I usually speak my mind, and call things by their right names. Your mental labor is of a kind not likely to improve the mind, or elevate the soul. It partakes too much of late hours; too much of cards and the dice-box; too much of strong liquors, sir. You are what the world calls a fast man, you are on the road to ruin and disgrace; you are traveling fast; you will reach your destination soon.

Mes. M. Dubois, this language to me is insulting; is unexpected, unmerited, uncalled for. You are an old man and your age protects you. I, sir, am a gentleman, and expect to be treated as such.

Dub. He who claims to be a gentleman, and expects to be treated as such, must conduct himself as such. In my estimation, the life of a gambler, a libertine, and a drunkard, is not compatible with the life and character of a gentleman.

Mes. [*excitedly.*] Have a care M. Dubois, or your gray hairs will not long protect you; I shall not endure this.

Dub. Be patient with me, M. Mesnard, as this will

probably be our last interview. Your way of life is fully known to me, and I will no longer appear to give countenance to it. I have repeatedly urged you to pursue a different course and warned you of the consequences of your present life. Now I shall have done with you. I can no longer retain your services In dismissing you I do not feel that regret I should were you a poor man, or had you a family dependent upon you. You have resources of your own, which, if properly improved will give you a competence; but they are fast being squandered. Let me intreat you to change your course of life. Be frugal; be economical; forsake the ways of depravity and of vice and become indeed a gentleman.

Mes. M. Le Maire, your advice is uncalled for. You indeed speak the truth when you say that I have other resources than the position I have held by your favor affords me. I am not dependent upon M. Edward Dubois, the Maire of Solenthel for either the necessaries or the luxuries of life. My fortune is at present ample, and I shall enjoy the world in spite of the sermonizing of M. Le Maire. [*turns up.*]

Dub. M. Mesnard my feelings toward you are those of kindness. I would have been your friend, but you have forfeited my friendship. I wish you well In half an hour Jarvais will be ready to give you the balance due on your account. He is now absent on business which will not detain him long.

Mes. [*Sarcastically.*] Thank you, M. Dubois. [*aside*] I'll be revenged for this. [*Exit* C. D. L.

Dub. [*Solus.*] Small hope of reformation there. Well, I feel a consciousness of having done my duty. The public welfare must be looked to.

[*Rings bell. Enter* DENNIS C. D. L.

Dennis. Did you ring your honor?
Dub. Yes, I rang.
Den. And was it me you was wanting?
Dub, Yes, I wanted you, or I should not have rang for you.
Den. Ov coorse you wouldn't, but what will I be doin' now?

Dub. Have you heard how the sick man is, at the foot of the hill?

Den. Yes, your honor, he's betther nor he was, and he's gettin' betther all the time. The ould woman says he'll be out agin in a day or two.

Dub. They are very poor, are they not?

Den. Indade they are your honor, and they would have suffered, but some kind soul, heaven save him, has conthrived to supply them with necessaries, and comforts; but they don't know who it is.

Dub. Do you know the widow who lives at the corner of the next street?

Den. Sure an I do, and I think poor creature, she has a hard time of it since she was left a widdy with two little childer.

Dub. Here, take this letter to her, and mind you don't let her know where it comes from.

Den. Trust me your honor; It's Dennis O'Grady that can kape a sacret shure. [*aside*] I wonder what the ould man has been writing to the widdy about.

[*Exit* C. D. L.

Dub. The widow will feel happier when she receives what is enclosed in that letter.

[*Enter a Servant* C. L. D.

Servant M. Henri de Pierrepont.

Dub. Show him in.

[*Servant shows in* DEPIERRE—*and retires.*

Dub. Good day M. DePierrepont.

DePierre. Good day M. Dubois. I met M. Jarvais, your Secretary, on the street a short time since, who informed me that you wished to see me on business of importance. I am at your service.

Dub. Pray be seated. [*they sit*] Henri dePierrepont I never look upon you but I am reminded of your father, my old friend; a man of scrupulous honesty, upright and just. In him you have had a good example, which I have no doubt you have copied to advantage.

DePierre M. Dubois your remarks concerning my dear departed father are just. His example was a worthy one, and I have endeavored to the best of my ability to follow it. It is my highest ambition that my life may be as pure as his, and that I may ever merit that respect which he commanded here.

Dub. You follow the business of a collector of rents I am told.

DePierre. Yes, M. Dubois, I have a wealthy uncle who furnishes me with some employment in that way.

Dub. Excuse me, M. DePierrepont, if I seem to inquire too closely into your affairs, but I have a great regard for the son of an old friend and may be able to do you a favor. I presume the income you receive as your uncle's collector is not large, and possibly you would not object to adding to it in an honest way?

DePierre. Good M. Dubois, it is true that my income is not large, and does not afford as many comforts to my little family as we might desire, yet it is sure and we are economical. I should not refuse an additional source of income if an honest one, you may depend.

Dub. I thought you would not. I have lately had some trouble with my collector, M. Mesnard, and have dismissed him. He was not the man for the place; his habits were not such as would command confidence. I have sent for you to offer you the position which is now vacant. Will you accept it?

DePierre. This is a great and unexpected favor you show me, M. Dubois; I should be very foolish to refuse it. I will do my best to serve you, and to give you confidence in my integrity.

Dub. [*rising.*] M. DePierrepont, you may consider that you do me a great favor, and relieve me of a load of anxiety, for I feel that I can trust you. Call here to-morrow and Jarvais will instruct you in the details of your position, and you may at once enter upon your duties.

DePierre. Thank you, M. Dubois; I will attend upon him. Good day. [*Exit* DePierre, C. D. L.

Dub. That business is settled to my mind. That Pierrepont is an honest fellow; he carries it in his countenance. He knows the need of prudence and economy. This good fortune will give new joy to his

wife and child. There is nothing that delights me so
much as to make worthy people happy.

[*Exit* DUBOIS, R. H. 1st E.

[*Enter* JARVAIS, C. D. L.

Jar. Well, M. Dubois has rid himself of a serpent
in Mesnard. He is a most villainous fellow; there is
murder in his eye. I wouldn't trust him with rents or
taxes, not I. But the good old Maire is so unsus-
pecting. He is not at all like me. I can see clear
through a man. I can tell a rascal when I meet him.
He has made a good exchange. Henri DePierrepont is a noble fellow and will honor the position.
Mesnard is a rascal; he carries it in his face. They
say the devil is always near when you are talking
about him, and here he comes.

[*Enter* MESNARD, C. D. L.

Mes. [*coldly.*] Good day, M. Jarvais.

Jar. Your servant, M. Mesnard.

Mes. I was directed by M. Dubois to meet you
here to receive a small balance due me for past services. I presume you have been informed of it?

Jar. I understand. I have it here. [*Takes a pack-
age of notes from his pocket-book and gives* MESNARD.]
You will find it all right I think.

Mes. [*Examines notes.*] Correct. [*Sneeringly.*] So
your frugal and economical master thinks me too
fast a man for the position I have held?

Jar. And has dismissed you—well?

Mes. Yes, he has dismissed me. But where does
he expect to find a better man; one that shall be his
ideal of purity and virtue?

Jar. He has already found one, who no doubt will
answer his expectations.

Mes. Indeed; may I inquire his name?

Jar. Henri DePierrepont. [*Turns up stage.*]

Mes. DePierrepont, a paragon of virtue truly.
[*aside.*] This is not the first time he has crossed my
path. No matter. I blame him not for this. But old
Dubois, the miserly economist, who has taken this
means to humiliate and disgrace me shall yet feel the
power of my hate. He has roused a devil in my

breast that calls out for revenge. Yes, M. Dubois, the time will come, I will be even with you yet.

[*Turns up.*]

Closed in in one.

SCENE 2.—A VILLAGE STREET IN ONE.

[*Enter* DENNIS O'GRADY, L. H. *with letter.*

Den. That master of mine is a queer old chap. He's always sending me round on all sorts of errands and telling me not to say anything about it. He has been a good master to me sure, ever since I turned up in this outlandish country. It was a poor boy I was, and nothing better than a tramp when I left ould Ireland and went to say. And after driftin' about in forrin countries I was ship-racked and cast away on the coast of France, and I didn't know where I was at all, at all. I wandered about widout a penny in my purse, and I wondered what ould Biddy O'Grady would say to know the sorry spalpeen, her poor fatherless boy had become, when I fell in with ould Mister Dubois and he took me in and became a father to me, and put me in his sarvice, and its a happy lad I've been ever since. Och! there comes Mister Maynard looking as sour as a vinegar barrel. He's got something on his stomach that doesn't set good. I wouldn't wonder if the ould masther has been giving him his ticket of lave.

[*Enter* MESNARD R. H.

Mes. [*excitedly.*] Curses on him, the tight-fisted old miser.

Den. Maning who an' you plase Mister Maynard?

Mes. Not you, you meddlesome Irishman.

Den. And it isn't me you mane, and it's well for the loikes of ye that it isn't. I'm a meddlesome Irishman am I? Well, if I be, I'll tell you something I heard a man say in a play onct. "Curses are like young turkey gobblers, and they'll always come home to roost." Take care they don't roost on you, Mister Maynard.

Mes. Fool! who asked your advice.

Den. It's good to take a fool's advice sometimes, Mister Maynard.

Mes. I would be alone.

Den. Well who's hindering ov ye? The strate is wide enough, and I didn't ax for your company.

Mes. Idiot! Vagabond!

[*Exit* MESNARD, L. H.

Den. Good day, Mister Maynard and take care the curse don't choke you; bad luck to you for a black-guard that you are. And sure it's a idiot, and a vaga-bond I am to be wasting my time talking to the likes of ye, when I should be carrying the masther's letter. I wonder what ould masther has been writing to the widdy.

[*Exit* DENNIS, R. H.

SCENE III.—CIRCUMSTANCES. *Scene.—A neatly furnished old fashioned room in M. Henri DePierre-pont's cottage. Old fashioned fire place* C *in flat. Practical door in* F. L. H. *Latticed window in flat.* R. H. *Table set for supper.* R. C. *Four high backed chairs Low stool on, Old fashioned sofa.* L. H.

A LAPSE OF TWO YEARS.

Discovered—MARIE DEPIERREPONT *seated* R *of fireplace.* MADELEINE, *aged seven years, on low stool beside her.*

Marie. Well, my darling, everything is ready for supper and your father will soon be here. So you have had a pleasant time, and enjoyed yourself with your playmates to-day?

Madeleine. Yes, mamma, we did have a real nice time.

Mar. Well I know you are tired my little one, but you will sleep all the better for it.

Mad. I want to ask you a question mother, about something that happened to-day.

Mar. What is it, darling?

Mad. Mother, what is a miser?

Mar. Why, my child, what put it into your head to ask such a question as that?

Mad. When I was playing on the street this afternoon with the other little girls, M. Dubois came along and they said he was an old miser, and all seemed to be frightened and ran away.

Mar. Did you run, too?

Mad. No, mother, he looked so pleasant and so good that I wasn't afraid, and he came up and spoke to me, and called me a good little girl. He said he knew my father, and that he would make me a handsome present when Christmas comes.

Mar. You was a good little girl not to be rude and show disrespect to M. Dubois, as the other little girls did. You must always respect him, for he is a good man, and has done a great deal for us.

Mad I thought a miser was something bad, because the other girls seemed so frightened. I don't believe M. Dubois is a miser, do you mother.

Mar. A miser my dear, is one who loves money and hoards it up and worships it. One who not only neglects to help those that are in need, but deprives himself of the comforts of life, that he may increase his wealth. M. Dubois is a prudent and economical man, and although quite rich, he deprives himself of many luxuries and lives in a very plain manner. He is not proud, like some rich men, and he does a great deal of good to those who are in need, but he is so odd and peculiar in his way, that those who are assisted by him seldom know who their benefactor is. M. Dubois is not a miser, my dear, but many think him one.

Mad. I have heard father say that M. Dubois has been very good to him.

Mar. Yes my dear, two years ago he gave him a position as collector, and since that time we have had many comforts which we could not have before. And M. Dubois has promised to do much better by him soon, as he has formed a strong attachment for him because your grandfather and M. Dubois were great friends.

[HENRI *passes window in* F.

Mad. Oh! here comes father. [*Jumps up and*

runs to the door to meet him.] Oh! my good father.
[*Enter* HENRI DePIERREPONT, D. F.

DePierre. What my little one, glad your father
has come? You have been a good little girl to-day, I
know you have. And you, Marie, my love, God
bless you. [*kisses her.*] How pleasant it is after
the cares and perplexities of the day, to come to such
a happy home, and be greeted by the happy faces
of you, my wife and daughter. This is indeed a
happy home, and you are my household treasures.
Thanks to good M. Dubois for the many comforts
we have been enabled to add to it. May it be ever
thus and may the precious peace and love which now
reign here, continue unbroken for many, very many
happy years to come.

Mar. Amen. Heaven grant it. But come Henri,
our supper waits.

DePierre. Yes, that must be attended to.
[*They seat themselves at table.*

DePierre. [*To* MADEL'NE.] Well, my darling what
have you found to amuse you to-day?

Mad. Oh! I have had nice times.

Mar. Madeleine has been playing with some of
the little girls to-day, and they have told her some
queer things about M. Dubois.

Mad. Yes, papa, they told me M. Dubois was a
miser.

DePierre. [*To* MARIE.] And you have taught her
better, my love?

Mar. Indeed, I have Henri.

DePierre. I thought so once, myself; but did the
people of our village know the good old man as I
do, they would have a very different opinion of him
from that generally expressed.

Mar. But Henri it is so good to have you with us.
I feel such relief after your long journeys, and do
you think it, many times I have fears for your safety.

DePierre. Why so, my love? What is there to
fear?

Mar. You know that your business as collector
often compels you to have large amounts of money

in your possession, which is liable to excite the cupidity of others. You might be waylaid, robbed and murdered for your money.

DePierre. There is no ground for such fears, my love.

Mar. And do you know that I have sometimes thought of Mesnard, the profligate and unprincipled person who was dismissed by M. Dubois and whose place you now hold; that he might seek to be revenged on you. I have heard that he is a most desperately wicked character, and would not scruple to take the life of any one that had crossed him.

DePierre. Marie, my love dismiss such phantoms, let them not prey upon your mind and rob you of the happiness you can enjoy. There is indeed no call for fear; ours is a peaceful and quiet neighborhood The whole country around us is filled with honest and industrious people, who would scorn to covet what is not their own. Their honor is my safeguard.

Mar. True ; but Mesnard.

DePierre. He went to Paris two years ago, where I hear, he is spending his life and fortune in dissipation. Depend upon it, our quiet village has no attractions for such as he; and as for revenge, he can have no cause for seeking it of me.

Mar. Well, no doubt such fears are groundless, but sometimes they will force themselves upon me, strive as I will to shake them off.

Madeleine during the foregoing dialogue has fallen asleep. MARIE *places her upon sofa* L. H. *A knock* D. F.

DePierre. Come in.   [*Enter* DUBOIS D. F.

DePierre. What! M. Dubois? Why, you are indeed welcome. Sit you down. [*They sit.*] It is seldom you honor our humble home with your presence.

Dub. It is not my nature, M. Henri DePierrepont to make many visits except upon matters of business I am somewhat peculiar; odd you may say; some even call me worse than that. But some know me better, Eh? What say you DePierrepont?

DePierre. It is true they do; that I can vouch for
M. Dubois.

Dub. A matter of business brings me here to-
night, something in which you can be of great service
to me.

DePierre. Say you so, Monsieur! You may always command my services.

Dub. You are aware DePierrepont, that I am a
large contractor; I am at the present engaged in tl e
construction of public works. I am also building a
church and a schoolhouse.

DePierre. I am aware of this, M. Dubois.

Dub. I have a large number of men in my employ,
and am frequently in receipt of money with which to
pay them. I have just received notice that a remittance of seventeen thousand francs awaits me at Bazeilles. It is not far, and to-morrow afternoon I propose to walk over and receive it. I would like your
company. I always prefer walking to riding when
the distance is not great; besides it is a healthful ex-
ercise you know; and as most of the money will be
in notes, it will not be weighty, consequently no
impediment to our journeying on foot.

DePierre. I will accompany you with pleasure, M.
Dubois.

Dub. On our return I propose to stop at the Soliel
d'Or for rest and supper. I shall be liberal, believe
me.

Mar. But M. Dubois would it not be more safe for
you to take a carriage while traveling with so much
money.

DePierre. My wife is worrying herself about rob-
bers; like all good women, anxious for her husband's
safety.

Mar. I think it is best always to be on the safe
side if we can.

Dub. Why my good woman what have we to fear?
With a kind Providence above us, and M. DePierrepont here, by my side, we shall be as safe as here in
your own cottage. The distance is not great, the
country through which we must pass is thickly in-

habited by an honest and industrious peasantry, and we shall travel it by daylight; so give yourself no uneasiness or anxiety; your husband will return all safe, and we shall enjoy many happy years together yet. The matter is all settled, so good night. Kiss the little girl for me, and tell her that I shall remember her when Christmas comes. [*Goes toward door in* F.]

DePierre and Marie. Good night.   .

Picture.

END OF ACT FIRST.

ACT SECOND.

SCENE I.—*A room in the Soliel d'Or.   Door in* F. *practical* R. H. *above* 1*st grooves.   Table and two chairs* L. H. *above* 2*d grooves, set for supper; all old fashioned.   Candles lighted on tables.*

Discovered.—MESNARD *disguised, seated at* R. H. *table.*

Mes. Two years have passed since I left Solenthel disgraced and humiliated by the miserly old Dubois, who hates a little enjoyment and harmless dissipation because it costs money, which he loves better than he loves the comforts and pleasures of life. I feel sure no one will recognize me in this disguise. I do not wish particularly to be known, as my business is not of a character to bear close investigation. I am not so well to do as I was two years ago. A gay life in Paris has made heavy inroads upon my fortune. I must find means to replenish my losses. Perhaps an opportunity may offer to draw upon old Dubois. I should not hesitate should such opportunity present itself. I am sufficiently desperate, I owe him an eternal hatred, and will yet be revenged for his insults. Here! Landlord. [*Rings bell.*]

[*Enter* DUMONT, L. H.

Dumont. Your servant, Monsieur.

Mes. Are you the landlord of this hotel?

Dum. Yes, may it please you Monsieur. How can I serve you?

Mes. Can you give me a supper?

Dum. Yes, Monseiur at once. What shall it be?

Mes. You look like a man of taste. I will leave it to your judgment.

Dum. Thank you, Monsieur. I think I can suit you.

Mes. Bring it here, upon this table.

Dum. Yes, Monsieur.   [*Exit* DUMONT, L. H. •

Mes. Evidently this fellow does not recognize me, nor suspect who I am. I will draw him into conversation. I may obtain some information of value.

Re-enter DUMONT, *preceded by a waiter with supper on a tray, which he arranges on table before* MESNARD *and retires.* DUMONT *is about to follow.*

Mes. Stay Landlord, don't be in such a hurry to leave.

Dum. No hurry Monsieur, only I thought you would prefer to eat alone.

Mes. Not I Landlord; a little social chat with your food sometimes helps digestion.

Dum. I have heard so.

Mes. Yes. Come sit down. [*Dumont sits* C.] You have a retired place here.

Dum. Quite so, Monsciur.

Mes. I should judge you were expecting travelers to-night?

Dum. Oh, Monsieur; we are always expecting them; that is our business.

Mes. I see you have a table prepared for supper yonder, which would indicate that you are expecting some particular ones.

Dum. Oh, Yes, Monsieur; I am preparing supper for two gentlemen who were to have been here long before this on their way to Solenthel.

Mes. I presume you are not troubled much with travelers in this retired place?

Dum. Not so much as I might wish, but notwithstanding I am fairly patronized. M. Dubois employs a large number of men at the village, and many of them visit us. They pay pretty well, and are quiet and orderly.

Mes. No doubt. Who is this M. Dubois of whom you speak? His name sounds familiar to me.

Dum. You are a stranger in these parts it would seem?

Mes. Me—ye—yes, I am from Paris, traveling for my health and to see the country. But M. Dubois?

Dum. M. Dubois is the Maire of Solenthel. He is a rich proprietor and contractor ; rather a strange character. Some call him a miser, he may be for all I know to the contrary; but he never passes this place without stopping, and patronizing us liberally.

Mes. I have heard of him, he handles large sums of money and receives large amounts from Paris and elsewhere, I believe?

Dum. And one thing is very remarkable about him. He never uses his carriage when he can perform the journey on foot. We are expecting him here to-night. It is something unusual for him to be so late ; he is always very prompt in everything. Something must have happened to detain him so long beyond the time of his appointment.

Mes..And who is his companion?

Dum. M. Henri DePierrepont, his collector ; a man in whom he has great confidence.

Mes. Henri DePierrepont ; indeed? I have heard of him likewise.

Dum. [*rising.*] Have you? Well I think I hear travelers without and I must go and look to the supper. [*aside.*] Zounds, I don't half like the looks of that fellow. He seems to have heard of every-body. I wonder if he ever heard of me before? He's got a sort of a corkscrew twist to his eye that I don't like. I'll tell the butler to look after the spoons. [*Exit* DUMONT, L. H.

Mes. So old Dubois is expected here to-night? This is indeed fortunate. Heaven truly favors me, and throws him in my way. To-night I may have an opportunity to wipe out some old scores, M. Dubois.

[*Enter* M. DUBOIS, *with bag of silver, and* HENRI DEPIERREPONT D. F. DUMONT *enters from* L. H. *and goes up to meet* DUBOIS.

Dum. Welcome, Welcome, M. Dubois; we have waited a long time for you. What detained you?

Dub. We have had a heavier load than we bargained for; this bag of silver is load enough for a horse. What say you, Henri?

[Mesnard listens attentively.

DePierre. It is something of a burden truly; but there are many that would gladly relieve you of it, M. Dubois.

Mes. [*aside.*] A bag of silver. More good fortune I must contrive to relieve the old man of his burden before he travels much farther.

Dub. Besides our burden there was some trouble at the ferry that detained us, and with the detention and the burden I am as hungry as a bear, and shall do ample justice to your supper, landlord. Let us have it at once.

Dum. It shall be here instantly; seat yourselves at the table which has been prepared for you.

[DUBOIS *and* DEPIERREPONT *seat themselves at table*, L. H.

Dub. And landlord bring me a bottle of Madeira.

[*Exit* DUMONT, L. H.

Dub. It is seldom I drink anything, but after the fatigue of the day, I must be a little liberal. What say you, Henri?

DePierre. Please yourself, M. Dubois; but you must be discreet. You know you dislike dissipation.

Dub. But there are times (they seldom come with me however) when a little stimulant may be beneficial.

Mes. [*aside.*] The old hypocrite. But no matter if both of them should get drunk, it would simplify my work amazingly.

During the foregoing dialogue the waiters have brought in the supper and wine and placed them on the table where DUBOIS *and* DEPIERRPONT *are seated.*

DePierre. [*Finding no knife calls.*]Waiter! Oh, he has gone; he has forgotten to lay me a knife; but here are two forks instead. No matter, I won't call him back. I have a good knife of my own which will answer every purpose   [*Takes a clasp knife from his pocket opens and uses it.*]

Dub. You see Henri, I promised you a good supper to-night, and mine host of the Soliel d'Or has done justice to my orders. Now lay to and do justice to what has been provided. I know you must have an appetite after our journey.

DePierre. My appetite is good, M. Dubois, depend upon it. I will do my share in disposing of mine hosts' provisions.

Dub. [*drinks wine.*] This Madeira is remarkably fine ; try some.

DePierre. No thank you ; I am unused to it, and to-night I feel a greater responsibility than usual resting upon me, and will not indulge.

Dub. Well, do as you please ; it is very fine.
                                [*drinks.*

DePierre. [*aside.*] M. Dubois is unused to wine, and I am fearful he may be overcome after the great fatigue of the afternoon. I shall need to keep my wits about me. I don't half like the looks of that stranger ; he has watched us with unusual interest, yet he may be honest for all that.

Dub. Why Henri, my boy, you do not eat ? certainly your appetite cannot have left you suddenly.

DePierre. I was thinking.

Dub. Of what ? Nothing serious, surely. I hope you have no trouble on your mind.

DePierre. [*hesitatingly.*] I was thinking that as we have got some distance to travel—

Dub. Oh, I understand you are afraid I shall drink too much wine—never fear—never fear—I shall be all right. But come let us finish our supper.

DePierre. Oh, I am not much given to fear ; and at present we are in safe quarters.

Dub. You're right Henri, my boy. They say I'm an old miser, I don't look much like one now. Eh DePierrepont ?

DePierre. No, no, my dear M. Dubois, but I am afraid the the wine is too much for you ; and I think with the large amount of money you have with you, it would be safer to hire a carriage for the remainder of our journey.

Dub. [*slightly affected.*] Nonsense Henri; no fear about the money. Nobody about here wants my money. Don't be afraid Henri, don't be afraid my boy.

DePierre. [*aside.*] Heavens the wine affects him more than I had suspected. The stranger overhears him and appears to be deeply interested. Should he be.—— No, no, he is doubtless an honest traveler.

Dub. Hire a carriage, Henri! Oh, no, that would never do; we can manage well enough. The carriage would be a needless expense. I should be laughed at in Solenthel. They would say the strict sober old Maire had broken down and had to be brought home drunk. No, no, that would never do; no, no; we'll go back as we came. Here, landlord!

[*Enter* DUMONT, L. H.

Dub. Your bill, landlord.

Dum. (*presenting bill.*) Here it is Monsieur.

Dub. (*examines bill.*) All right, Landlord. (*hands money to Dumont.*) I see you have been quite liberal in your charges. Come, Henri, we must be gone. [*rising.*]

Dum. But you don't think of leaving at this late hour, M. Dubois?

Dub. Why not, Landlord?

Dum. (*cautiously.*) You know, Monsieur, that you have a large amount of money with you, and you are fully two miles from home.

Dub. Well, what of that? The people about here are honest; we have no burglars nor highwaymen lurking about. What have we to be afraid of? De-Pierrepont is strong and able; he is a match for any single man that might attack us; and as for me, old as I am, I'm no baby. We will go. Come, DePierrepont.

DePierre. But had you not better take a gig?

Dub. Nonsense, Henri; let us begone. It is true the wine did begin to have some effect upon me, but I had sense enough to stop. It has all gone now.

I am all right. The fresh air will drive away all bad effects. Come, let us go. Good night, Landlord.

[*Exit* DUBOIS, DEPIEREPONT *and* DUMONT D. E.

Mes. (*rising.*) They have gone and I will follow shortly. (*discovers DePierrepont's knife which he has left on table where he and* DUBOIS *had been eating.* Ho! What's this? DePierrepont's knife, and on it his initials; another lucky circumstance. I will appropriate it. The Landlord will never miss it, and as for DePierrepont his mind will be too much occupied to-night to think of it again. I dare not attack the two. DePierrepont is more than a match for me; but I will shadow them until they separate, and then for my revenge. I will settle with the Landlord and then quietly depart. This is a lucky circumstance.

closed in one.

SCENE SECOND.

the opportunity.

SCENE.—*On right half flat, Cottage with practical door. On left half, village street. Night. Lights down. Dark stage.*

The exterior of DEPIERREPONT'S *Cottage.* "*The Opportunity.*" *Music Pizz. Enter* MESNARD, *cautiously* R. H.

Mes. This is DePierrepont's cottage. They will pass this way. Perhaps they will separate. I will conceal myself and watch my opportunity.

Music Pizz. MESNARD *retires* L. H. *When he is off enter* DUBOIS, *carrying bag of silver and* DE-PIERREPONT R. H.

DePierre. Well, M. Dubois, you have carried that bag far enough; let me relieve you awhile.

Dub. Yes, you may relieve me now, for here is your home. You shall take the bag in and keep it until morning. I will go the rest of the way alone. *Gives bag to* DEPIERREPONT.

[*Enter* MARIE *from door in Cottage.*

Marie. (*Goes to* DEPIERRE.) I heard your voices, So you have returned all safe? It is very late; yet it is such a relief to my mind to see you safe again. I have been very anxious about you to-night, Henri.

DePierre. And Madeline !

Marie. She is asleep, poor child.

DePierre. Well, you see we are safe, Marie; and now I will accompany M. Dubois to the top of the hill and return immediately.

Dub. Nay, DePierrepont; I can go the rest of the way alone : it is only a short distance, so you keep the bag till morning, and I'll send a cart around for it. [*Laughs.*

DePierre. But M. Dubois.

Dub. Nay; Henri; I will not hear of it; I insist; so go you in with your good wife, and leave me to go alone.

Marie. But M. Dubois, will you not come in and rest awhile?

Dub. No, my good Madame DePierrepont, I do not need it, besides it is late, and I will go on at once So good night and God bless you. [*Exit* DUBOIS, L. H. 1st *entrance.*

Depierre and Marie. Good Night.

Marie. There goes a good old man.

DePierre. Yes, you say true. Heaven bless him.

Marie. But what detained you so late, Henri?

DePierre. Come in and I will tell you all. I am sorry I allowed him to go alone. Well it must be so. Come in, the night is chilly, and you'll take cold standing there. [*Exit into cottage.*

[*Music Pizz. Re-enter* MESNARD *cautiously* L. H.

Mes. It is as I had wished. Old Dubois goes alone and goes to certain death. The opportunity has come and Heaven itself throws him within my power. Now, M. Dubois, the hour for my revenge has come.

(*music. exit* L. H. 1st *entrance.*]

SCENE III. (THE CRIME.)—*Open landscape near the residence of* DUBOIS. *Night, Lamps down. Dark Stage. Enter* DUBOIS, L. H. 1st *entrance.*

Dub. Well, I am almost home ; my weary journey is well nigh over. Soon I can rest. Yet I regret exceedingly that I did not allow DePierrepont to accompany me. I have a strange feeling coming over me; an unaccountable sense of dread and danger. I am unused to such feelings, and why they should overpower me now I know not. It is nothing—what should I fear? There is a kind Providence over me that has hitherto protected me from all harm. In a moment more I shall be home again. (*Turns up stage.*) *Music.* MESNARD *enters* L. H. *steals upon* DUBOIS *suddenly and stabs him in the neck with* DE-PIERREPONT'S *knife.*

Dub. Help! Murder! (*falls.*)

Mes. Behold! Mesnard; him whom you insulted and humiliated. He now has his revenge !

Dub. (*faintly.*) Oh villain—may heaven—I die.

[*Dies.*

Music. Agitato pp. MESNARD *robs* DUBOIS *of his money, watch and rings.*

Music. Agitato p. Distant noise of voices without L. E. U.

Mes. Ha! the old man's call for help has alarmed the neighborhood. This knife will throw the pursuers off the scent and fix suspicion on DePierrepont. [*He lays knife beside the body.*] I must be gone at once. With the proceeds of this night's work I can retrieve my fortune. And now farewell to Solenthel. Farewell to France forever. [*Exit hastily* R. H.

Music Agitato Forte.

Enter JARVAIS *and villagers* L. H. U. E. *with lights.*

Lights Up.

Jar. I heard a cry for help. What could it mean ? M. Dubois has not yet returned. [*Discovers body.*] Ah! What is here? A bleeding body—What? M. Dubois, and dead !

Omnes. M. Dubois! Murdered !

[*All gather around the body.*

Jar. Yes, murdered for his money. [*Sees knife which he picks up.*] Here is a bloody knife. He has

been murdered and robbed.   Alas, my good old master; who could have done this deed?

PICTURE.

Plaintive music till drop is down.

END OF ACT SECOND.

ACT THIRD.

SCENE I.—*The Accusation.   Interior of DePierrepont's Cottage, same as Scene* III *Act* I. *DePierrepont,
Marie and Madeleine discovered.   Bag of silver on.*

Marie. Your journey yesterday Henri, was a weary
one.

Henri. It was indeed; that bag of silver was a
heavy load to carry such a distance.

Marie. And you will rest to-day, will you not?

Henri. I have nothing to call me away, and I think
I will remain at home, and for one day enjoy the society of my good wife and my darling Madeleine.

Mad. Oh, Father, I am so glad you are going to
stop at home.

Henri. So you love to have your father stop at
home, do you, my little one?

Mad. Indeed I do, my good father.

Henri. Well there's a kiss, my darling [*kisses her*]
but I can't be always with you.

Marie. And I am glad likewise, Henri; it is so
seldom we have you with us during the day; it will
be indeed a great pleasure.

DePierre. No less to me my darling.

Marie. Does it not seem strange that one so well
able to ride as M. Dubois, should travel so much and
so far on foot?

DePierre. It is his peculiarity, his oddity I might
say; and I am fearful that it may some day cause him
serious trouble.   I trembled for him last night when
he persisted in coming on foot at so late an hour,
after having taken more wine than is usual for him;
and it had seemed to affect his judgment slightly.

Marie. M. Dubois seldom drinks wine I believe?

DePierre. Seldom. He is very temperate in his habits and although he is an old man, his health is remarkably good and his constitution unimpaired. I like his ideas of temperance and frugality.

Marie. I have heard that it was on account of his intemperate habits, he dismissed the former collector M. Mesnard.

DePierre. That is true. M. Dubois is a kind hearted man, and is good to those of whom he has reason to think well. We must overlook his oddities.

Marie. Most assuredly we must.

DePierre. A walk of ten miles now and then, to please him, will not do much harm. It is singular he has not sent for this bag of silver this morning; he is always so punctual. No matter, if he doesn't send soon, I will carry it to him. [*a knock* D. F.] Ah, some one knocks. It must be his messenger. Come in !

[*Enter* JARVAIS *and* LAROQUE D. F. DEPIERREPONT *rising to meet them.*

Good morning M. Jarvais, you are welcome, and your friend be seated. How is M. Dubois after his journey of yesterday. [JARVAIS *averts his face.*

DePierre. Why M. Jarvais you turn away; you do not speak ; your looks betoken some great sorrow. What has happened ? Speak ! M. Dubois—

Jar. Is dead !

DePierre and Marie. Dead !

Jar. Yes, dead !

DePierre. Great Heavens ! How? What? He left me last night in his usual health and spirits.

Jar. He has been murdered !

DePierre. Murdered ?

Jar. Yes, robbed and murdered !

DePierre. By whom ?

Jar. I cannot answer that question M. DePierrepont, I am too much shocked to give utterance to the fearful tale. This gentleman M. LaRoque agent of police, will answer for me.

LaRoque. M. Henri DePierrepont, I have a very painful and unpleasant task to perform. Yesterday

you accompanied M. Dubois to Bazeilles on foot.
There he received a remittance amounting to seventeen thousand francs. Returning late at night you
stopped and took supper at the Soliel d'Or, where
M. Dubois drank more than was usual, and when
you left together he was somewhat under the influence of wine. This is all that is known of you and
M. Dubois, till at a late hour M. Jarvais heard a cry
for help, near the residence of M. Dubois. He
aroused some of the neighbors, and on searching
they found the venerable Maire within a few rods of
his own house, lying dead and bleeding.

DePierre. Merciful heavens! who could have done
this deed? Why did I not accompany him?

LaRoque. On examination it was found that his
watch, ring and money had been taken.

DePierre. It was for his money then, that he was
murdered?

LaRoque. So it appears. On further search a
knife was found near him, open and bloody; and
upon it the initials H. D. P. !

DePierre. Amazement! My knife! How came it
out of my possession? Ah! I remember; I used it
last night at the Soliel D'Or. I must have left it
there, or dropped it on the way.

LaRoque. M. Henri DePierrepont, the most unpleasant duty is yet to be performed. You were the
last person seen with M. Dubois. The knife with
which the murder was committed belongs to you;
circumstances all point to you as the guilty party;
and in the King's name I arrest you for murder.

A file of Gens de Armes enter D. F. *and form across
the back of the stage.*

DePierre. What! Me! I the murderer of M. Dubois?

Marie. [*frantically.*] No, no, no; he is innocent.
I know he is innocent. I can prove it. I can swear
it.

LaRoque. Woman, circumstances are too strong
against your husband and my duty is too plain. M.
DePierrepont where are the seventeen thousand

francs M. Dubois had with him last night? Also his watch and ring?

DePierre. I know not, on my soul I know not. When we parted last night, here at my own door, he left in my charge a large bag containing one thousand francs in silver; there it is, [*points to bag.*] He promised to send for it in the morning; this is all I know. Of the murder, who committed it, or of the sixteen thousand francs M. Dubois had with him, I know nothing. I am accused of his murder. What possible motive could I have to kill that good old man? He was my friend, my benefactor. I coveted not his money. What cruel fate is this that has surrounded me with such fearful circumstances?

Marie. Oh, sir, my husband is innocent. I know it. I can prove it. Surely my testimony should be received. As you have said, he went yesterday with M. Dubois to bring the money of which you have spoken. He arranged with him in my hearing to stop at the Soliel d' Or for supper. At a late hour last night they returned. I saw them both just outside the door of this cottage. My husband insisted upon accompanying M. Dubois home, but he would not allow it. He left with him this bag of silver, and said in a pleasant manner he would send a cart · around for it in the morning. I heard all this; I saw M. Dubois depart on his way alone. My husband and myself entered the house together, and he has not been absent since. I know it; I swear it; so help me heaven. He is innocent of this murder.

LaRoque. Madame, you are an interested party, and your testimony can have but little weight against the terrible circumstances that surround your husband; and if it could I am not the person to listen to it. I am but a servant of the law, and must perform my duty. Your husband must go to prison and await the action of the court.

Marie. Is there a righteous judge above us? and can it be that truth and innocence plead in vain? M. Jarvais to you I speak; you have known my husband from a child; can you believe him capable of the horrible crime of which he stands accused?

Jar. Madame DePierrepont I am astounded; overwhelmed with confusion and regret to think that I, an old and faithful secretary of M. Dubois, should have recommended so strongly to his confidence a man who could take advantage of his generosity to become his assassin. I would willingly believe your story if I could, but the circumstances are too overwhelmingly against him.

Marie. You too, M. Jarvais, have you lost confidence in us? you that I never would have believed could doubt our uprightness and truth. To whom then can we look for sympathy and hope?

DePierre. Marie, my love, my wife, this is a sad ending to our dreams of happiness and peace. We must look above to a higher, wiser power than man, to unravel this dark mystery, and break the meshes of this fearful web of circumstances which fate has thrown around me. Madeleine, my darling child, come to your father's arms. [*Takes* MADELEINE *in his arms.*] God bless you dear ones. God bless you both. [*kisses them.*) I must leave you now. Let us hope that when this matter is heard before a court of justice, as it must be, the bright sun of truth will pierce the dark, o'ershadowing cloud that has so suddenly overwhelmed us. Let us hope that the real assassin may be discovered and we restored to happiness.

Marie. God grant it.

LaRoque. Forward! [*The Gen de Armes face to the left.*]

Marie. Oh, cruel fate! [*Falls on DePierrepont's neck.*]

Mad. [*kneeling to LaRoque.*] Oh! please don't take my father away.

Music.   Picture.

Closed in in one.

SCENE II.   STREET IN ONE.—*Enter* DENNIS O'GRADY, L. H.

Den. Faith, Dennis O'Grady, an its bad luck you

are havin' agin.   It's your ould luck, and the fat's all
spilled in the fire.   The ould masther is dead, and its
a sorry day for you Dennis, you unfortunate spalpeen.
It's murdered he is, bad luck to the villain that did
the dirty job.   And what will ye be doin' now?   Jest
as you get somebody to be a father to you, and give
yez a home for life, to have him killed entirely and
you cast out on the wide world an orphan.   You'll
have to go to say agin, Dennis, you blackguard, and
be saking your fortin in forrin parts.

[*A noise of female voices as if hooting or deriding
some one* R. H.]

Och ! what's the maning of all that noise?   What's
the matter now? [*looking off* R. H.]   There's a regu-
lar rumpus.   Why, there's Misthress Parepong and
her little girl ; and it sames as if every woman in the
nayborhood was hooting of them.   I wonder what its
all about.

MARIE *rushes on excitedly with* MADELEINE, R. H.

Mar.   My poor child, why are we pursued and per-
secuted thus?

Mad.   Mother, why do those angry women follow
us, and call you a murderess?   I'm sure you never
killed any one.

Marie.   Oh, my poor child, you do not understand.
These people believe that your father killed M. Dubois and that I was his accomplice, because I insisted that he was innocent, and have tried in court
to save him.   They seem determined to drive us
from the village.   Where can we look for shelter and
protection? [*Seeing* DENNIS] Ah Dennis, do you
hate and despise us too?

Den.   Faith, Misthress Parepong, Dennis O'Grady
is not the boy to turn his back upon a woman in
trouble.   They say that your husband murthered my
masther, ould Mr. Dubois ; but I'm not so clare
about that myself.   Sure and it looks mighty bad for
him, but I can't get it through my thick skull, at all
at all.   But if he did do it, its no rasin' why they
should be mistreating you about it.

Marie.   And you don't think me capable of being

the accomplice of a murderer?

Den. Faith and I do not. And I make bould to
say that I believe you're too good a woman, and your
husband, too, heaven help him, for any such mur-
therin business.

Marie, Thank heaven, there is one that has some
sense of justice.

Den. Justice is it? And faith and its Dennis
O'Grady doesn't belave there is any justice in perse-
cuting a poor lone woman and a darling little rose-
bud of a child, because the head of the family has
been unfortinate. Old Misther Jarva and myself
don't justly agree on these pints, so I've taken my
lave of him and if there is anything I can do for you,
to help you, just say the word and its Dennis O'Grady that won't go back on ye.

Marie. We have started to go to the court-room
to see my husband, possibly for the last time on
earth; and these infuriated women, who should have
shown me friendship and sympathy, have pursued,
taunting and reviling me. I have just escaped them.

Den. Faith, ma'am and I'll go with you and see
you safe; just you go along with the little girl, and
I'll stand betwane you and harm.

Mar. Thanks, good friend. Come, my darling.

[*Exit* MARIE *and* MADELEINE L. H.

Den. Faith it's meself that has the greatest res-
pict for the female sex, but when a woman turns into
a she tiger and goes into the strates to brawl and
hoot at her nabors, it's a sorry bit of respect she'll
get from Dennis O'Grady. Of all the divils in the
wide world, a she divil is the worst.

[*Exit* DENNIS, L. H.

Change.

SCENE III.—A COURT ROOM.

The Sentence.

. *Bench for judges* C *back. Jury box and seats for
jury* L. H. *Prisoner's dock* R. H. *Tables and Chairs
for Counsellors, Officers of the Court, etc.*

Discovered. President of Court on bench with two Associate Judges, President in Centre. Twelve Jurymen in places, Counsellors, Attornies, Officers of the Court, Soldiers, and male and female villagers.— HENRI DEPIERREPONT *in prisoner's dock.* JARVAIS *and* LAROQUE *on with spectators.*

President of Court. Henri DePierriepont, you have been tried according to law by a jury of your countrymen. The evidence has been of a strong character, but entirely circumstantial. There has been so much of mystery surrounding it, that although the jury have found you guilty, yet in view of the extreme penalty of the law which is death, they have hesitated, and have recommended you to the mercy of the court. What have you now to say why sentence should not be passed upon you?

DePierre. May it please the honorable court, I am innocent of the crime with which I am charged; as innocent as you yourself. It were easy to say this you will reply, and I must freely admit that almost any one in my situation would say the same, even though guilty. I cannot blame the court, nor the officers of the law, that I stand as I do, in the position of a convicted felon. A most cruel fate has thrown around me a cloud of circumstances, which even the light of truth cannot at present penetrate ; yet, I have confidence to believe that this mystery of the murder of one of the best men will one day be solved ; and it will then appear as clear as sunlight, that I am innocent ; truly innocent ; and have suffered a most cruel wrong. This trouble has come upon me so suddenly, so unexpectedly, that it has almost deprived me of the faculty of thought; and it is but little I can say to weigh against the testimony already given. The circumstances of my journey with M. Dubois to Bazeilles and return, are as testified to up to the time of reaching my own door; but there we separated. I have not seen him since, and know nothing of the murder, save from the statements of others. I had no motive

for murdering the good old man ; he has always been
kind to me ; a generous friend. I did not covet his
money; he had made my circumstances easy. I am innocent; but my wife is the only person except the real
assassin that knows me to be innocent. All except my
wife and child, and the good landlord of the Soliel d'
Or, believe me guilty. This is indeed hard to bear,
but not so hard as to know that my wife because she
has shown herself a true and noble woman, and has
testified to what she knows to be true, is looked upon
as my accomplice in this crime ; that the people of our
village, to whom she should look for sympathy and
kindness, have turned their backs upon her and despise her, and my child ; my darling Madeleine is
looked upon and treated as the daughter of a murderer. This is too horrible ; too great a punishment ;
it is worse than any sentence the court can pass upon
me. I have done. [*His feelings overcome him, and
he sinks back exhausted into his seat.*] *A pause.*

Pres. [*arising.*] Henri DePierrepont stand up—
The court has listened to you with patience, and all
that now remains is to pronounce upon you the sentence of the law ; which in consideration of the recom-
mendation of the jury, is that you be condemned to
the gallies and to hard labor for life. Remove the
prisoner.

DePierre May it please the court ; as I am about
to be taken hence, grant me an opportunity to say a
few words and bid farewell to my poor wife and innocent child. There is but little prospect that I shall
ever see them again this side of the eternal world.

Pres. The officers will allow you ample opportunity
before you are taken away, to speak with your wife
and child.

A file of soldiers enter L. H. *and form across the
stage. Judges, Jurors, Attendants, Councillors etc.
Exeunt* R. H. U. E. *leaving Officers, Soldiers and Gen
deArmes. Spectators retire* R. & L. *1st Entrance.*

Enter DUMONT *with* MARIE *and* MADELEINE L. H.
DEPIERRE. *leaves dock and comes to meet them by per-
mission of Officers in charge.*

DePierre. Marie my love, how strange, how fearful sometimes are the ways of Providence. Only a few short days ago we were happy in each other's love; no thought of such a scene as this; not a cloud over-shadowed us, and we were looking forward to years of prosperity and peace. But now how changed; what an avalanche of horror and despair has been hurled upon us; it is too horrible to conceive of its reality. I, though innocent as this darling child, stand here convicted of murder; and though spared the extreme penalty of death; doomed to a felon's life of toil. And you my devoted wife, looked upon by all that were your friends and neighbors, as acces-sory to the crime. And even you my darling inno-cent little one, despised and shunned as the child of a murderer. But I must submit to cruel fate and leave you, perhaps forever.

Marie. [*clinging to* DEPIERRE.] Oh, say not that fearful word forever. No, no, no, no, my heart will break at the bitter thought.

DePierre. Let us pray that it may not be. Let us hope that some good angel that now hovers over us and knows the truth of this dark mystery, may yet find some instrument through which to make it known. Till then we can only trust in that Provi-dence which overlooks all things.

Marie. It is hard to trust, when such cruel wrong is allowed to go on.

DePierre. True, it is hard; yet doubtless there is some good design hidden beneath this darkness. What to say I know not. Could I find words to com-fort and to cheer you, I would speak them. I know you have expended all our little accumulations for my defence in this trial, and henceforth your lot will be a hard one, and it will require all your fortitude to bear up under it. Where you should look for friends to find nothing but scorn and contempt is indeed a hard lot; and I am powerless to aid you. I need not ask you to cherish my memory when gone; that would be to distrust the pure devotion you have al-ways shown. Never while life shall last, no matter

what the trials and sorrows we are called upon to
suffer, can we forget each other, and my darling
Madeleine, may that God who is the father of the
fatherless, watch over, guard and bless her. She is
yet too young to realize this fearful situation as she
may hereafter. Do your best to rear her in the ways
of virtue and truth, that her life may be a walking,
living denial, of the foul aspersions the evil minded
will cast upon us. Teach her never to forget that
her father, though a victim of cruel circumstances, suffered for no crime. [*To* M. DUMONT.] You, M.
Dumont, have been our friend in all this great trouble.
It is beyond my power to reward you, but heaven
will bless you for the efforts you have made to save
me.

Dumont. I am rewarded sir in the consciousness
of having done my duty. I have been satisfied of
your innocence, and regret that my efforts have failed.

DePierre. Ah Marie, you will sadly need protection when I am gone.

Dumont. M. DePierrepont, I fully appreciate the
position in which you leave your wife and child, and
depend upon it, I shall do all in my power to render
them friendship and protection from insult.

DePierre. I believe you M. Dumont, I believe you.
I know you have a kind heart. Yet, I am fearful that
the feeling will be too strong for you to content suc-
cessfully against it here. Doubtless they will be com-
pelled to leave Sclenthel.

Dumont. I will do my best.

[*The file of soldiers face left and open in centre.*]

DePierre. The guards await my departure. Marie
my love I must go. I must utter that last bitter
word, farewell. [*To* MADELEINE.] Farewell darling ;
God bless you ; pray for your poor father that he may
come back soon ; good bye. [*Hands* MADELEINE *to*
M. DUMONT *and goes up and takes his place with the
guards.*] Farewell, may heaven protect you.

Marie. No, no. This is too much ; all is lost. [*Faints.*

Plaintive music. Picture. Slow Drop.

ACT FOURTH.

REMORSE.

A Lapse of Fourteen Years.

SCENE.—*Grounds of M. Gaillard in the suburbs of Lima, Peru. A magnificent garden scene. On* R. H. *a fine portico, with steps down to the stage, being the entrance to* M. GAILLARD'S *house. Rustic seats. Garden chairs. An easy chair* R. C.

DENNIS O'GRADY *discovered arranging things.*

Den. And so they say the masther's failing badly, and what if he should die now; just as I've got so nicely settled in a new and comfortable home. It's jest your ould luck Dennis, to be living till everybody else is dead. I never shall forget about ould Mr. Dubois, the kindest ould masther I ever had; and he went and got killed and left me a poor orphan, and poor Mr. Parepong and all the rest of the family had to suffer for it. It was fourteen years ago. I wonder will it ever come out right? I got sick of the outlandish counthry with the crooked jaw-breakin' names, and went to say again, and finally turned up down here in South America and hired to a new masther. He isn't the agreeablest I ever saw, but he has always been ginerous with me, and I hope it isn't going to be dying that he is and leave me an orphan the second time. Here comes the Docther and I'il ax him all about it.

[*Enter Physician from house* R. H.

Physician. Good morning, Dennis.

Den. Your sarvint, Docther dear. And how is the Masther this mornig?

Physician. He is very poorly, Dennis.

Den. And don't you think you can cure him Docther? And it's sure you'll have the blessin' of Dennis O'Grady if you do.

Physician I am fearful, Dennis that he will never be any better.

Den. Sorry day for you Dennis, you unfortunate spalpeen. What would Biddy O'Grady say if she only knew the throuble you're always in.

Physician M. Gaillard wished me to send you to him, as he had a message for you to deliver.

[*Exit* PHYSICIAN L. H.

Den. A message is it, faith then and I must attend to it. Oh, you're an unlucky dog with your masthers Dennis O'Grady. [*Exit into House* R. H.

[*Enter* ARTHUR DeVERSAN, LaROSE *and* CLEVEL R. H.

LaRose. M. Gaillard has a fine estate ; these grounds are indeed beautiful.

Clevel True, LaRose, and it would seem that their possessor might enjoy unalloyed happiness in such a paradise.

LaRose. And yet M. Gaillard is not happy. He does not seem to enjoy life.

Clevel. But you know M. Gaillard is a bachelor. He lives a life of single blessedness, which to my mind is a condition anything but blessed.

LaRose. You are right Clevel; man was not made to live alone; in such a condition he can never more than half enjoy life, for he is but half what God intended him to be.

DeVersan. Gentlemen, your remarks would seem to be aimed at me as well as M. Gaillard, my worthy patron. I too, am a bachelor, and yet I think I more than half enjoy life. But perhaps my youth may excuse me in your eyes.

LaRose. Say rather your devotion to M. Gaillard, who feels that through the intervention of the ordinance of matrimony he has been separated from all his friends except you ; and he regards you with jealousy fearful that you too may be induced to enter the matrimonial state, and he be left friendless.

DeVersan. You forget gentlemen that M. Gaillard was not always single. He has tried the married state, and from what he has told me, I should judge that his experience in that direction had not been altogether as pleasant as yours seems to have been

He certainly has not felt desirous of thrusting his neck into the matrimonial noose again.

LaRose. I was not aware that M. Gaillard had ever been married.

Clevel. Nor I. Is it true, DeVersan?

DeVersan. It is true. You know that for the past six years I have been his legal adviser and confidante

LaRose. It would seem DeVersan that you have had most gloomy company in M. Gaillard; he seems so sullen and morose at times, and always grave and thoughtful.

DeVersan. It is true, M. LaRose, there are times when he is morose, and even sullen; and he appears like one whose mind is weighted with some heavy burden, yet he has been very kind to me.

Clevel. Yes, DeVersan, you have undoubtedly found a good friend in M. Gaillard.

DeVersan. True! Seven years ago I came here a poor young man to seek my fortune. I had studied law, and started as a lawyer. At first my prospects seemed gloomy enough, but becoming acquainted with M Gaillard, he employed me, and soon became greatly attached to me. Through his influence I have been very successful.

LaRose. You are a lucky dog, Arthur. You have found a real El Dorado in your patron, M. Gaillard. Well you are a good fellow and deserve your success.

Clevel. And I also rejoice in your good fortune and hope you may find a partner to share it with you.

DeVersan. Oh, I understand your meaning perfectly, but I have no thought of changing my condition. I have seen nothing yet that could make an impression upon my heart.

LaRose. Perhaps DeVersan has left his heart in sunny France.

DeVersan. Now, gentlemen, this is too bad, you are two to one; don't be so severe upon a poor bachelor. I assure you I came here with a whole heart, untouched by Cupid's arrow, and although for the last half hour you have deliberately aimed to set me against my single life, you have failed. Depend upon it when I do fall in love, it will be a sudden affair. But let us leave this senseless talk, and turn to something more serious. M. Gaillard has not been seen in public much of late. His health is very feeble; he has grown prematurely old; and his system seems to be breaking up. He visits his garden daily for an airing; but seldom goes beyond its limits.

LaRose. Do you think he is on the decline?

DeVersan. It may be, yet I think there is something more than physical infirmity wearing upon him.

Clevel. He is very rich.

LaRose. And has no relatives. Should he die DeVersan, you will be likely to receive something handsome.

DeVersan. Gentlemen, it ill becomes us to stand here discussing the probabilities of profiting by the death of a fellow being. M. Gaillard with all his failings, has been very generous, and when he shall depart hence, which, pray heaven, may not be for a long time to come; there are many that will lose a good friend.

[*Enter* DENNIS *from house* R. H.

Den. [*having overheard the foregoing speech.*] And you may well say that, Mr. Versong. It's meself that knows what you say is true, and if the masther should die, its Dennis O'Grady that wouldn't have a dry eye in his head at all.

LaRose. I meant no harm; DeVersan; you know it is the way of the world to discuss the probabilities as to what disposition the wealthy will make of their property at death, especially if their chances for life are not good.

Den. And it's a mighty mane world to be sticking its dirty nose into business that doesn't concern it, at all, at all.

DeVersan. Well, gentlemen, as I see M. Gaillard is not out at present, I will accompany you a short distance on your way and return anon, as I have some matters of business to communicate.

[*They are going* L. H.

Den. Hould on, Mister Versong, I want to spake a word to yees.

De Versan. Say on, Dennis.

Den. The masther sent me to find you, and when I found you I almost forgot my arrend, because you see, I didn't have to look for ye. The masther wants to see you for something important, he said; and he'll be ready to meet you here in the garden, in a quarter of an hour.

De Versan. I will attend on him.

[*Exeunt* LaROSE, CLEVEL *and* DeVERSAN, L. H.

Den. Now, then what will I be doing next. I must see that the chair is all right for the masther. [*Arranges easy chair.*] Now then I must go to the doctor's and get some pills for the master, and a bottle of physic for the ould gray horse that's got the masels or some other outlandish disase that I don't justly remember the name of now.

[*Exit* DENNIS L. H.

Enter GAILLARD *from house* R. H. *assisted by* FRANCOIS, *who helps him to chair,* R. C. *He sits.* FRANCOIS *stands* L *of* GAILLARD.

Francois. The air is fine and refreshing this morning, M. Gaillard.

Gaillard. Yes, Francois, to those who are susceptible to soothing influences, it is undoubtedly refreshing; but to me, nothing refreshes me now. I have grown old, weak and withered, a prey to disease; and with everything around me to make life desirable, I cannot enjoy it.

Francois. It grieves me good, M. Gaillard to hear you speak thus, and to realize that what you say is true. It seems hard that one who has been so good and generous as yourself, should be afflicted thus.

Gaillard. Talk not to me of goodness, Francois. Poor judges are we of each other. You call me good and generous, yet I would be willing to sacrifice all that I possess could I really have the satisfaction of feeling worthy of the good opinion yourself and others I have befriended hold concerning me.

Francois. I wish you would be more cheerful Monsieur, but the peculiarities of your disease are such as seem to deprive you of the enjoyment of pleasant influences; and to lead you to disparage your own self. Endeavor, Monsieur, to throw off these gloomy feelings and I have no doubt you will be yourself once more.

Gaillard. I fear it is too late Francois. Would I could be cheerful, but it is no use trying. I must suffer on. You may go now. [FRANCOIS *is about to retire.*] Stay! You watched with me last night, Francois?

Francois. I did.

Gaillard. Did you observe anything unusual?

Francois. You seemed disturbed and tossed about much in your sleep.

Gaillard. [*greatly agitated.*] I said nothing? You heard no talking, Francois?

Francois. You seemed at times much troubled in mind; you groaned heavily, and uttered low sounds as if in talk, but I could not understand the words uttered.

Gaillard. So, you are sure you heard nothing, Francois?

Francois. Nothing that I could distinguish or understand.

Gaillard. It is well; leave me for the present. I expect M. DeVersan here shortly on some business. When I need you I will call.

[*Exit* FRANCOIS, U. E. L.

Gaillard. So my secret is safe. Safe! Yes safe! 'Tis here; here; concealed within my breast to rankle here and torture still my soul. Oh! could I with one bold stroke, blot from my memory that fearful night. Coward that I am, I tremble lest in my very dreams, I may disclose to those about me the horrid record of that fearful crime. Oh, remorse; thou frightful, gnawing fiend that doth pursue my soul. Ceaseless the torture I endure. What is all this wealth to me? To those about me it hath a show of power, of greatness, but to me—it cannot buy me peace. 'Tis stained with blood. There's blood all about me. I cannot banish it from my sight. I cannot drive away the vision of that pale old man. I see —I see him now—he beckons me to come with him. No, no, no, I cannot go with you. Take him away. I faint—I—I suffocate! Help! Francois! [*faints.*]

FRANCOIS *enters hastily, goes to* M. GAILLARD *and raises his head. He slowly revives and looks around.*

Francois. Had I not better help you in?

Gaillard. [*Looking wildly around.*] Where am I? What! Francois, you here? Oh; I had forgot; I called you. Then I am still safe. He's gone. Did you not see him, Francois?

Francois. This is some strange fancy; there is no one here but ourselves.

Gaillard. Oh, I see—I see—I have been dreaming again. I feel better now. You may retire. [FRANCOIS *retires* L. U. E.

Gaillard. I cannot endure this agony. These fearful phantoms which pursue me, sleeping or waking-ere long will drive me mad. I am a broken down old man. I am very feeble and can live but a few more days at best. De Versan shall hear all. I will confess to him the guilty wretch I am, before I die, and thus if possible drive off these harrowing spectres from my mind.

Enter DEVERSAN. GAILLARD *arises to meet him but sinks back exhausted into chair.* DEVERSAN *assists him.*

DeVersan. Why M. Gaillard, you seem very weak to-day. You alarm me; can I be of any assistance to you?

Gaillard. DeVersan I have had a very bad night, and to-day I am very poorly. You have come in good time; sit you down. I have important business that I must transact with you while I have yet the strength. [*Very feeble.*

DeVersan. [*sits.*] I hope M. Gaillard your illness has not taken a serious turn. Perhaps the information I imparted to you yesterday has been too much for you in your feeble condition.

Gaillard. Perhaps that has precipitated matters somewhat. Possibly you cannot conceive of the motives which led me to commission you to obtain the information you yesterday imparted?

De Versan. I have not divined them.

Gaillard. Listen to me, then judge; Arthur De-Versan listen to a dying man, and interrupt me not while I reveal to you a tale of horror that shall chill your blood. You see before you an assassin, a thief, a murderer. Sixteen years ago I was a Collector of Taxes, and adjoint to the Maire of Solenthel, in the Department of Ardennes, in France. The Maire was that same M. Dubois concerning whom you instituted inquiries. He was a rich man and reputed to be somewhat miserly. My habits of life were such that he became justly incensed against me and I was dismissed. His language to me I considered insulting, and the dismissal humiliating; I vowed to be revenged. I was then possessed of an ample fortune; but leaving Solenthel, a gay life in Paris soon made heavy inroads upon it, and two years later I returned greatly reduced in cirumstances, and sufficiently wicked to commit robbery, and even murder to improve my finances and compass my revenge. I was so disguised that no one could recognize me. Sitting one evening in a little hotel not far from the village, I saw two men enter and call for supper. One was M. Dubois; the other Henri DePierrepont, the man who had succeeded to my position. While they were eating I discovered from their conversation that they had with them a large amount of money. A dreadful thought came over me, that here was my opportunity for me to retrieve my fortune and accomplish my revenge. DePierrepont, on departing, left behind him a knife which I secured to aid me in my devilish work. I followed but dared not attack both at once, as I knew DePierrepont was more than a match for me. Once or twice I thought of giving up my fearful design; but at the house of DePierrepont they separated and Dubois went on alone. I bounded after him. I gave myself no time for thought; I stabbed him in the neck; left the knife beside him; robbed him of his watch, ring and money; then fled. I left France forever. I came hither under the assumed name of Gaillard, I became a merchant; rich; respected; but I never knew a happy moment. Not only had I murdered M. Dubois, but Pierrepont was suspected, tried, convicted, and sentenced; only not to death. I thus ruined an honest man and sent his family forth from society to suffer as outlaws.

DeVersan. Oh! horror! Wretched man, what a tale of guilt is this.

Gaillard. DeVersan, listen to me, my friend; do not turn from me, in this, my extremity. I have left you my sole heir.

DeVersan. Never will I—

Gaillard. Hark! You must, and you will. Take my property and think when you enjoy it, with pity on its present guilty owner; and I will make public confession; pay the heirs of Dubois the amount stolen from them, and by proving my own guilt, obtain the pardon of the innocent DePierrepont. Refuse me and I will die impenitent, for my last friend will have deserted me.

DeVersan. I accept for the sake of those that have been so deeply wronged, and that you who have been so good a friend to me, may be able as far as possible to purge your soul from this awful crime.

Gaillard. DeVersan, my dear friend, you take a heavy load from off my soul. Francois!

[*Enter* FRANCOIS, L. U. E.

Gaillard. Summon instantly the Consuls of France and England, some clergymen and the Alcalde.

[*Exit* FRANCOIS *into house* R. H.

Gaillard. And you, DeVersan, go and call some of your French and English friends; and in their presence I will make full and free confession of my guilt, and may Heaven have mercy on me.

DeVersan. [*turning.*] Amen.   [Picture.

END OF ACT FOURTH.

ACT FIFTH.

SCENE FIRST.   THE CONVICT'S DAUGHTER.

SCENE.—*The forest of Ardennes. Wood in Two.
Cut wood in one.*

MADELEINE DEPIERREPONT (*age 22) discovered.
Before her is a bundle of sticks which she has been
gathering. She is poorly but neatly clad.*

Plaintive music as curtain rises.

Madeleine. Still the same weary round of toil.
Still — still an outcast. No friends to cheer and
comfort; no word of kindness, save from her who
shares with me my woe, my mother dear. Crushed
and oppressed; all gone. But hope still clings to
me, and gives some vague and indistinct assurance
that all will yet be well. Last night I dreamed of
my dear father, who for fourteen years has passed a
life of unrequited toil. I dreamed that he was free
and that he clasped me in his arms, and kissed me as
fondly, as tenderly as when I was a child. Oh. that
heaven would grant that one precious boon, to see
my father free once more and the black stain re-
moved from off our lives. 'Twas but a dream and I
must still toil on.

[*Music.*]—*She is about gathering up the wood to depart when* ARTHUR DEVERSAN *enters* R. H. 1st E.
*He is in a riding suit, with whip in hand, as just
alighted from horseback.*

DeVersan. What ! A female here alone in this
wild forest ? [*aside.*] She's as handsome as a picture. Young woman, what brings you to this solitary place?

Mad. Please you Monsieur, I am not so solitary
as you would suppose. I have a friend not far away.

My mother dwells in yonder hut which you can see
through the trees [*points off* L. U. E.] and as you ask
me my business I think there may be no harm in
answering. I have been gathering wood to cook our
dinner.

De Versan. [*Looks off* L. U. E.] What a miserable
abode and what a wretched occupation for so pretty
a girl. Surely my dear you might put your fingers
to better use. Here's that will buy you firewood for
months to come. [*Tosses a piece of gold to Madeleine.*]

Mad. Surely, Monsieur, I have done nothing to
give you the right to insult me. What you have done
may have been meant kindly, but I ask alms of no
one.

De Versan. [*slightly confused.*] Pardon me, mad-
amoiselle, I meant no insult; pardon me I pray you.
I thought you poor, and my impulse was to aid you.

Mad. Thank you, Monsieur, for the first kind
words I have heard these fifteen years except from
my own mother. But go your way, else the whole
country will shun you too.

De Versan. What mean you?

[*Music. Hurry and chord.*] *Enter* EDWARD DU-
BOIS R. H. *greatly enraged with upraised whip, and
approaches* MADELEINE.

Edward. Begone wretch! Viper! begone and dare
not speak to an honest man.

De Versan. Amazement! What can this mean?

Mad. [*to Edward.*] [*calmly.*] I did not speak to
Monsieur. Monsieur spoke to me.

Edward. Raise your accursed lips to me, and I
will scourge you with my whip.

Mad. [*with spirit.*] Perhaps M. Edward Dubois
is a coward.

Edward. [*advancing.*] What! dare you answer?

[*He is about to strike her; De Versan prevents him.*]

De Versan. Nay, Edward you would not strike a
woman.

Edward. [*in rage.*] A woman! Do you call Mad-

eleine DePierrepont, the child of the murderer of my
uncle Dubois a woman ? say rather a fiend.

DeVersan. [*greatly agitated.*] What! Madeleine
DePierrepont! [*staggers;* EDWARD *supports him.*]
Madeleine DePierrepont! Is that Madeleine DePier-
repont? No, she is not a woman—

Mad. Another enemy. [*Exit hastily with wood,*
L. U. E.]

DeVersan. No, she is something more noble.

Edward. Why so much interested in one so hate-
ful to me?

DeVersan. How can you manifest such bitter
hatred to one so lovely? To me it is a mystery.

Edward. Shall I tell you her history.

DeVersan. I have heard it already but did not expect to find her here.

Edward. She dwells in yonder hut with her mother, where for fifteen years they have been outcasts
from society, shunned and scorned by all the country around.

DeVersan. And you too Edward, join in this perse-
cution against two weak and suffering women, believ-
ing the father guilty; which to me is not clearly
proved and you know I am a lawyer. Why; the wild
savages of North America are more civilized than
you. I see in this heroic couple subjects of wonder
and admiration, but not of hate. Poor creatures!
Fifteen years of suffering and misery have not satisfied you all, but you must still treat them as outcasts.

Edward. DeVersan you have just come from America, where, it appears, you have picked up strange
notions. For my part, the wife and daughter of an
assassin, and the assassin of my uncle are detestable
wretches whom I must ever hate.

DeVersan. Injustice, infamous injustice I think
I see her meek face now, looking at me so proudly
and yet so sweetly. I never saw anything so lovely
in my life.

Edward. Why, the man is in love, ha, ha, ha.

[*Laughs.*

DeVersan. Half. And what is more, Edward, do

you know I would marry that girl to-morrow if she would have me; but I know she would not.

Edward. By my faith, DeVersan, you amaze me; and you know I am not easily amazed. Of course you are joking—?

De Versan. Time will show. But now my dear fellow, you follow that path in search of pleasure; I this on business.

Edward. Adieu till to-morrow.

DeVersan. Yes, you breakfast with me at the Soliel d'Or.

Edward. Agreed, my philosopher, to please you; naught else would induce me. I detest the place; the landlord, M. Dumont always insisted upon the innocence of DePierrepont and protested against what he is pleased to call the injustice shown to Madeleine and her mother.

De Versan. He is right and I like him for it.— While I remain in this neighborhood he shall receive my patronage.

Edward. You are altogether too generous in your ideas of men and things.

De Versan. Think as you please, but be assured Edward Dubois, the time will come when you will deeply regret the harsh treatment you have bestowed upon these two friendless women.

Edward. I think you will be disappointed Arthur; but again adieu. [*Exit* R. H.

De Versan. [*solus.*] How weak is the judgment of such men. Did Edward Dubois know what I know, he would bitterly regret his sudden outburst of passion; his shameful manifestation of hatred and rage toward that unfortunate young woman. Poor fellow, what a pity he is not more enlarged in his ideas. But he shall know all to-morrow. How singular that I should discover in an old friend that I once knew in Paris the nephew of old M. Dubois, the murdered man, and the heir to his estate. Ah! Edward, I have a surprise in store for you. It is very strange what an impression that beautiful young woman has made upon me. Hitherto Cupid's darts have fallen harmlessly about me, but it would seem that the thoughtless expression I made to my two friends in Lima, Peru, is about to be realized. "When I fall in love it will be a sudden affair." Ha, ha, ha, There is no mistake, I really am in love. But I have business with this young woman and her mother. I have as great a surprise in store for them as I have for Dubois. I will go at once, make known my mission, and my love, and learn from them my fate.

[*Exit* L. U. E.

SCENE SECOND.

[*The Mystery Solved.*]

SCENE.—*Interior of a charcoal burner's hut in the Forest of Ardennes.*

A rude, semi-circular interior composed of poles tied together at the top. The crevices stuffed with mud and thatch. A rude fireplace C. *A rough door practicable in* F. R. *A rough bed in one corner. Two old chairs and small log on. An old table, cooking utensils, etc. Everything neat, but exhibiting the most extreme poverty.*

MARIE DEPIERREPONT *discovered sewing on coarse work, plainly, but neatly attired.*

Marie. [*pausing.*] Yes, 'tis fifteen years to-day since he was taken away from us. Still all is dark and the pale light of hope just flickers in the socket. Heaven seems deaf to prayer and supplication. I almost waver in my faith in power omnipotent and just. Still we must struggle, toil, and pine under the dark cloud of woe. Oh, God! in mercy hear; give us some light to strengthen us to bear the heavy burden cast upon us.

Enter MADELEINE D. F. *with bundle of wood. She appears greatly agitated. Throws wood down by fireplace.*

Marie. Madeleine, my child, what ails you? You seem greatly agitated.

Mad. Oh, mother! mother! Let us leave this place.

Marie. Why, my daughter, what has happened?

Mad. Even here in this lonely retreat away from
the haunts of human beings, we are pursued by those
who hate us.

Marie. What mean you?

Mad. Just now as I was gathering wood in the forest, two men on horseback stopped near me and dis-
mounted; one of them, a good looking stranger, ap-
proached and on seeing me, asked my business, and
threw me this piece of gold, saying I could put my
fingers to better use; this would buy me firewood for
months to come. I resented this as an insult. He
apologized and said he "meant no insult; his motive
was good, he thought me poor, and felt impelled to
aid me." I was thanking him for his kind words,
and would have returned the gold, but on the instant
the other, who was young Edward Dubois, came up
in a great rage, and flourishing his riding whip, called
me "a viper" and told me to "begone, and dare not
speak to an honest man." I replied, "I did not
speak to the gentleman, he spoke to me." This enraged him more and he threatened to scourge me
with his whip. Stung to anger, I hinted that he was
a coward. He became perfectly furious and would
have struck me had not the other prevented him;
who asked him if he was not ashamed to raise his
hand against a woman. Young M. Dubois foiled in
his purpose and livid with rage hissed out, "do you
call Madeleine DePierrepont, the daughter of the
assassin of my uncle Dubois, a woman? Say rather
a fiend." At the mention of my name a strange horror seemed to seize upon the other, and staggering
back into his companions arms he exclaimed "Madeleine DePierrepont! Is that Madeleine DePierrepont? She is not a woman." Hearing these words,
I hastened away grieved to know that another had
been added to the number of those that hate and
despise us.

Marie. Calm yourself my child; for your sake I am
grieved, for myself I have endured such treatment for
so many years that I may say I am calloused, har-
dened to it. The scorn of fifteen years has made me

despise the world; but you are hurt, and justly so, my child. Whither could we fly from here? Doubtless such an annoyance will not occur again. We know that young Dubois hates us, but he will rather shun than seek us here. Poor, misguided young man I hope the time will come when he will see his error. But come my child, build the fire, and make ready the dinner. We have no time to waste.

Mad. Yes, mother, I do not care for what young M. Dubois said, but I am vexed that the good looking stranger should have said I was not a woman.

[*Enter* DEVERSAN, D. F.

DeVersan. You are not a woman, but an angel.

Marie. What means this intrusion?

Mad. Why am I thus pursued.

DeVersan. You seem somewhat surprised. Madame; you will be still more so when I add that I have come here with the deliberate intention of imploring you to give me your daughter's hand in marriage.

Marie. Sir, this—

DeVersan. Oh, hear me, Madame! Not now, not instantly; but when you know me better.

Marie. [*indignantly.*] Monsieur, this is too much. Go! The felon's daughter is still too good for insult.

DeVersan. Perhaps, Madame, your surprise will cease when I tell you I have come sixteen thousand miles to prove it.

Marie. [*greatly agitated.*] You are—speaking—seriously?

DeVersan. On my soul and conscience.

Mad. [*grasping hand of* DEVERSAN.] Joy, joy, the saviour has come at last.

Marie. The clouds begin to break!

Mad. The light begins to dawn.

DeVersan. Be calm, my dear young woman, and I will tell you my story in a few words. You will then understand my motives in coming here. I scarcely expected to find you so near to Solenthel; but at last determined to try. I came here yesternight, and soon heard of your heroic courage and resignation.

Be seated, Madame, and you, dear girl, and listen to tidings that shall be joyful ideed to your filial hearts.

[*They sit.* MARIE *on chair* R. C. DEVERSAN C. MADELEINE *on log* L. C.

Marie. Thank heaven, our prayers are heard.

DeVersan. I am a young Frenchman, and about seven years ago I emigrated to Peru in search of fortune. I started as a lawyer, and through the aid of one M. Gaillard a merchant with whom I became acquainted, found business plentiful enough. I knew many Frenchmen in the place, but M. Gaillard was my most intimate friend. He was more than twice my age; grave; even sullen and saturnine; but he had quaint ways; was very charitable; and I liked him. Besides, the others were married; had families and he was alone. We used to meet of an evening at a cafe, play picquet; and then walk home together. He was very rich and lived in great style, but not in any way up to his income. People wondered he never married; but he said he had been married once, and was not inclined to repeat the experiment. He looked with alarm upon the prospect of my settling down in life, and did all in his power to reserve to himself one bachelor friend. Some over a year ago he was taken ill and his physician intimated to him that he could not recover. The disease seemed more of a mental than of a physical character; together with a general breaking up of nature, owing to a continual strain of mental troubles. During his indisposition he seemed strangely interested about the affairs of one M. Dubois, who was robbed and murdered at Solenthel some fifteen years ago; and commissioned me to make inquiries about the whole affair; which I did and acquainted him with the result. The effect upon him was to cause him rapidly to grow worse and sending for me suddenly, he confessed that he himself was the murderer.

Marie. Great heaven! The dawn has come.

Mad. Yes, yes, the mystery is solved.

DeVersan. He said his real name was Mesnard.

Marie. What! he that was a former tax gatherer and adjoint to the Maire?

DeVersan. The same.

Marie. After his dismissal he went to Paris and was never heard of again. How came he at Solenthel without being recognized?

DeVersan. After two years he came back disguised. He said that he felt keenly his humiliation and disgrace and resolved to be revenged. On the night of the murder he was present at the Soliel d'Or, when your husband and M. Dubois entered. From their conversatian, he learned that they had a large sum of money with them, which he resolved to obtain. When they left he followed them, having first secured a knife your husband left behind.

Marie. Then he did leave it at the Soliel d'Or?

DeVersan. He did.

Marie. How the dark clouds melt before the sun of truth.

DeVersan. After they separated at the door of your cottage, he pursued Dubois till within a short distance of his own house; rushed upon him from behind, stabbed him with DePierrepont's knife; robbed him and left the bloody knife for the purpose of turning suspicion upon your husband. He left France forever, but he could not flee from a remembrance of his crime. The horrid image of the murdered man was always before him tormenting a: d upbraiding.

Marie. How horrible this tale.

DeVersan. The recital filled me with horror. I could not speak. "DeVersan" he said, "turn nct from me in my extremity, I have left you my sole heir." I shrank from him with disgust, and refused to receive the wealth of a murderer. He insisted that if I did he would die impenitent; but if I consented he would make a public confession, pay the heirs of M. Dubois the money stolen; and by proving his own guilt obtain the pardon of DePierrepont. I accepted.

Marie. And may Heaven bless you for it.

DeVersan. An hour later, in the presence of the consuls of France and England, four Englishmen, four Frenchman, two priests and the Alcalde; Gaillard, or rather Mesnard, made his solemn confession, which was signed by all present, sealed, and one of two copies given to me. That copy is now in the hands of the Minister of Justice. And here young woman, here is a copy of your father's free pardon. (*showing paper.*

A wild exclamation of joy from both women.

DeVersan. [*Taking Madeleine's hand.*] And now, Madeleine, before I have a chance for rivals, may I renew my offer for your hand and heart?

Mad. M. DeVersan, no man on earth can do for me what you have done. In one short hour I have lived years of joy. That joy I owe to you. Give me back my father and the love and devotion of my whole life shall be yours.

DeVersan. And Madame DePierrepont, what say you now?

Marie. To this sudden resolution of my daughter I can only add my hearty approval.

DeVersan. To-morrow, then, your joy shall be complete. Meet me early at the Soliel D'or, where I have prepared a grand surprise for some of those who who have despised you. There Madeleine, you shall see your father, and you, Madame, your husband. Till then adieu.

Marie and Madeleine. Joy, joy, we'll meet you.

Picture.

CLOSED IN IN ONE.

SCENE THIRD.

SCENE.—*The forest of Ardennes. Wood in one.*

[*Enter* DENNIS O'GRADY R. H.

Dennis. [*solus.*] I wonder where my new masther can be. I have looked all over the counthry for him and he's nowhere to be found. His horse is tied out here all alone in the woods with the miskatoes, and nobody near the poor baste to keep him company.

I hope it's isn't robbed and kilt the masther is. Oh Dennis O'Grady it was a lucky day for ye's when your old masther died down in South Ameriky, and left all his property to Mr. Versong, and I was turned over wid the rest of the goods and chattels. Faith and is it goods I am? Is it good for anything ye are, Dennis, you blackguard, but to be losing your masther and getting cast adrift on the world. It was a mighty big load the old masther carried with him into the other world. And 'twas him kilt old Mr. Dubois, that made all the throuble for the Parepongs, and was the rason of my differin' with old Mr. Jarvais. Troth and he's gone the long journey; but he did a good sarvice at the laving, by making a clane breast of it; may Heaven be merciful to him. Och, here comes my new masther, and he isnt robbed nor killed at all, at all.

Enter DE VERSAN, L. H. *absorbed.*

Dennis. He seemed to be dreaming about something. I wonder had I better be wakin' him. I say! Mr. Varsong; is it there you are?

De Versan. [*observing Dennis.*] What! you here, Dennis?

Den. Faith and I am, and I've been hunting all through the woods for you. I found your horse tied to a tree, stamping his feet and busy wid his tail fighting the miskatoes, and I was afraid you had been robbed and kilt out here in this unlucky and outlandish counthry.

De Versan. So you found the horse busy with the mosquitoes?

Dennis. Yes, and he has nothing to ate but bushes.

De Versan. I declare, I was so absorbed in matters of business that I forgot that I had left the horse.

Dennis. Forgot the horse, did you? [*aside*] I wonder what's the matter with the master. he never forgot the horse before. I wouldn't wonder and he was in love. I knew a fellow that was in love onct, and he forgot to eat his breakfast for three days at a time.

De Versan. Well, Dennis, you was looking for me, anything wrong at the hotel?

Den. No, your honor; only I wanted to spake a word in private.

De Versan. Well, say on Dennis.

Den. May it plase ye, masther, I've been a sort of rolling stone all my life, drifting about on say and land, and it isn't much moss I've gathered at all. It's many a long year since I've seen or heard from ould Ireland and I know not if Biddy O'Grady, the mother of the vagabond Dennis, be living or dead; and as I have engaged you for my masther, and am under orders to go back with you to South Ameriky, when you are ready to lave, I want to ask you for lave of absence to go over to ould Ireland and see the ould mother if she be alive, and let her see the illegant and well-behaved gintleman her scapegrace of a Dennis has grown since he left the ould sod.

De Versan. It shall be as you wish, Dennis; you shall go back to old Ireland and carry with you sufficient money to make your old mother comfortable, if she be yet alive.

Den. May Heaven bless you, Mr. Varsong for a kind hearted gentleman, and may the favor of all the saints be poured upon you for your goodness to a poor sthray vagabond. I'll come back, Mr. Varsong and I'll stick to you and sarve you for life. Och, and wont I make the ould mother happy? I will [*makes extravagant demonstrations of joy*] [*pauses.*] But suppose the ould mother should be dead. Sure, and that would be a sorrowful day for you, Dennis O'Grady.

De Versan. Where have you been Dennis, since I left the hotel?

Den. On an errand for the landlord.

De Versan. An errand for the landlord, eh?

Den. Yes, sir, he wanted me to go and see old Mr. Jarvais and tell him to come 'round to-morrow morning.

De Versan. Did you see him?

Den. I did; and I told him all about the way things had come out, and I showed him that I was right all the time.

De Versan. Right about what?

Den. Why you see, Mr. Jarvais and meself had a difference of opinion about Mr. Parepong killin' the ould masther, and that was the rason I went to say, and you had the good luck to get me along with the rest of the goods and chattels.

De Versan. Indeed; Well Dennis I think I will walk awhile before I return. You go and take my horse.

Den. Take your what?

De Versan. My horse.

Den. Oh, your horse is it? Take your horse will I? And what will I be doin' with him?

De Versan. Why ride to the Soliel D'or.

Den. Ride him is it? And suppose he should throw me off?

De Veersan. What! Are you not used to riding?

Den. I am not! I never rode but onct in my life, and that was in a sarcus I went to before I left ould Ireland.

De Versan. And what did you ride there?

Den. A jackass. The man that bossed the show brought him out, and axed did any of the boys want to ride him. And faith said I, I don't mind if I thry, for he looked as innocent as the parish praste. So I got on his back and before I knew where I was, he rared up behind, and began to pitch and toss like a ship in a heavy say, and I was landed over among the benches, with a black eye and a bloody nose; and the man said why didn't you hold on? Hold on to what? says I. His tail sez he. And he wouldn't let me sez I. Then he called me a fool for trying to ride a donkey before I had learned; and I belave he was right.

De Versan. Well, if you don't care to ride the horse, you can take him by the bridle and lead him.

Den. Lead him is it? But suppose he wont follow me?

DeVersan. Oh, he'll follow you well enough.

Den. But wont the baste bite ?

De Versan. Oh no, he's as gentle as a lamb. Come along.   [*Exit* DEVERSAN, R. H.

All right, masther. I'll take the baste to the Solay de'Or, if he don't lay me so low I can't get there.
    [*Exit* DENNIS R. H.

SCENE FOURTH.

Re-united.

SCENE.— *A handsomely furnished apartment in the Soliel d'Or.*

Discovered.—HENRI DEPIERREPONT R. C. MARIE *on his right.* MADELEINE *on his left.* DEVERSAN L. C. DUMONT *at back.*

DePierrepont. Yes, my dear ones, once more united. Happy hour. Thank God that after fifteen years of toil and woe, we meet again to share each other's love. The night has passed, the morning breaks ; the sunlight bursts upon us, and gives me back my wife and child. And to you Monsieur, under Providence, we owe the happy solution of this great mystery. How can we ever repay the debt we owe you.

DeVersan. I am doubly repaid already. The plighted faith of Madeleine, supported by her mother and even now ratified by you, is a reward I had not thought of, or expected; when I left the distant shores of South America, to bear to you poor sufferers the happy solution of the Mystery of Ardennes.

DePierre. I feel M. DeVersan that I can entrust my daughter's happiness to none braver or nobler than you. You who have sacrificed so much of ease and comfort and have traveled so many thousand miles to rescue three poor outcasts, whom you might have left to suffer, while you enjoyed the murderer's wealth at ease; has shown you to be indeed a noble man, and worthy of my daughter's love.

DeVersan. I did no more than my duty when I redeemed my promise to the unhappy man, who was the cause of all these years of woe.

DePierre. Marie, my love, what a change these years have made. When I was torn away Madeleine was but a little prattling child; now she has grown to be a lovely woman; the image of her mother when first we met, Marie. And you, with all your toil and care have still found time to cultivate her mind and rear her up in truth and virtue.

Marie. Yes, Henri, I have done my best. As you predicted when on that dreadful day we parted, my lot has been a hard one, yet in all my struggles I have not forgot your last requests concerning her.

DePierre. And you too, good M. Dumont, did not forget these dear ones, when they were left friendless among their enemies, although it cost you no small sacrifice.

Marie. Yes, Henri, the secret aid of this good friend helped much to cheer our lonely life. We owe him a lasting debt of gratitude. Though all beside him, turned from us, he still maintained his faith that you was innocent.

Dum. M. DePierrepont, to me this is indeed a joyful moment. To see you restored to your family and friends makes me feel young again. Depend upon it I shall dance at Madeleine's wedding as nimbly as the liveliest in the village. I always suspected that mysterious stranger who took supper here on the night of the murder; and now it appears that he was none other than Mesnard, and the murderer of M. Dubois. I hope, now that you have returned, and the cloud of suspicion has been lifted from off you, that we shall long enjoy your society in Solenthel.

DeVersan. Good, M. Dumont, I am sorry that our arrangements are such that your friends cannot remain long in France. The death of M. Gaillard left me the sole owner of a large estate in one of the pleasantest spots on earth. Thither I must return; not as I had anticipated when I left, alone and a bachelor, but in my company her whom I shall shortly call my wife, my Madeleine. It is arranged that M. DePierrepont and wife go with us and there,

far from these scenes of toil and sorrow past, enjoy
the happy sunshine of the future. M. Dumont, nothing would give me greater pleasure than to have you
accompany us to our new home in South America.

Dum. Thanks, Monsieur, for your generous offer
but I am too old and too strongly attached to the
soil that gave me birth. Were I younger it might
be different. To those who have suffered so much
and so long, the change must be beneficial (*a knock*)
Ah! one knocks; it must be M. Jarvais, he has been
informed of the happy turn affairs have taken and
I have sent Dennis to accompany him hither. Come
in friends.

[*Enter* M. JARVAIS D. F. *assisted by* DENNIS. *He
is very old and feeble.* DUMONT *goes up and helps
him forward.*

Den. Masther Varsong; I've brought you a young
convert to the truth.

DePierre. Why my old friend Jarvais; I am glad
to see you here. How changed you are.

Jarvais. Yes, my dear DePierrepont, Im very feeble. I have lived to a great age—far beyond the allotted
time of man. I have just learned of your justifica-
tion and free pardon. Old and feeble as I am I
cou'd not rest till I came to congratulate you, and
humbly ask your pardon, and that of your good wife
and daughter for allowing my confidence in you to be
shaken. But the mystery, the fearful mystery, with
all its circumstances, blinded my eyes and warped
my judgment. But now all is clear, bright and cheerful. Thank God.

DePierre. My old friend, you have done nothing
that needs my forgiveness. God bless you, old man,
I only rejoice that Heaven has lengthened out your
span of life to behold this happy day.

Jarvais. God bless you Pierrepont, God bless you
Madame, and you too Madeleine. You have been
doubly blessed. I under-tand you've found your
father and a lover both. God grant it be a happy
union.

Mad. Thank you, M. Jarvais, for your kind wishes.

Den. And sure this is a blessed time all round, since ould Misther Jarvais and myself got reconciled And now Masther, I suppose I can go back to ould Ireland and hunt up the ould mother.

De Versan. To-morrow, Dennis, arrangements shall be made for your departure.

Dum. And now good friends, I must inform you that our breakfast waits us.

De Versan. Stay yet a little longer; there is one more to come, a specially invited guest. I think I hear his step without. Yes, here he comes.

Enter EDWARD DUBOIS D. F. *On seeing* DEPIER-REPONT, *his wife and daughter, he starts back and is about to leave in disgust.* DEVERSAN *grasps him by the wrist.*

De Versan. Stop, Edward; rather kneel and ask for pardon than attempt to fly. Read this man. [*Hands him a printed bill.*]

[*Reads.*] "DePierrepont's sentence"—unjust—fearful mistake—his free pardon—confession of Mesnard *alias* Gaillard, the murderer. Great Heaven! is this true? De Pierrepont, your hand. No apology can make amends for my conduct, but what I can do, I will. This bill will satisfy the whole country.

De Pierre. M. Dubois, you did but as others did; appearances were against me and you condemned me.

De Versan. Edward, my friend, in this you see the danger of judging from appearances. Had this noble man been truly guilty of the crime for which he was condemned and has unjustly suffered; his wife and child should have been pitied, not scorned. As it is, a wicked prejudice has made these two women outcasts for fifteen long years. And now, M. Dumont, our breakfast shall no longer wait.

CURTAIN.

END OF ACT FIFTH.